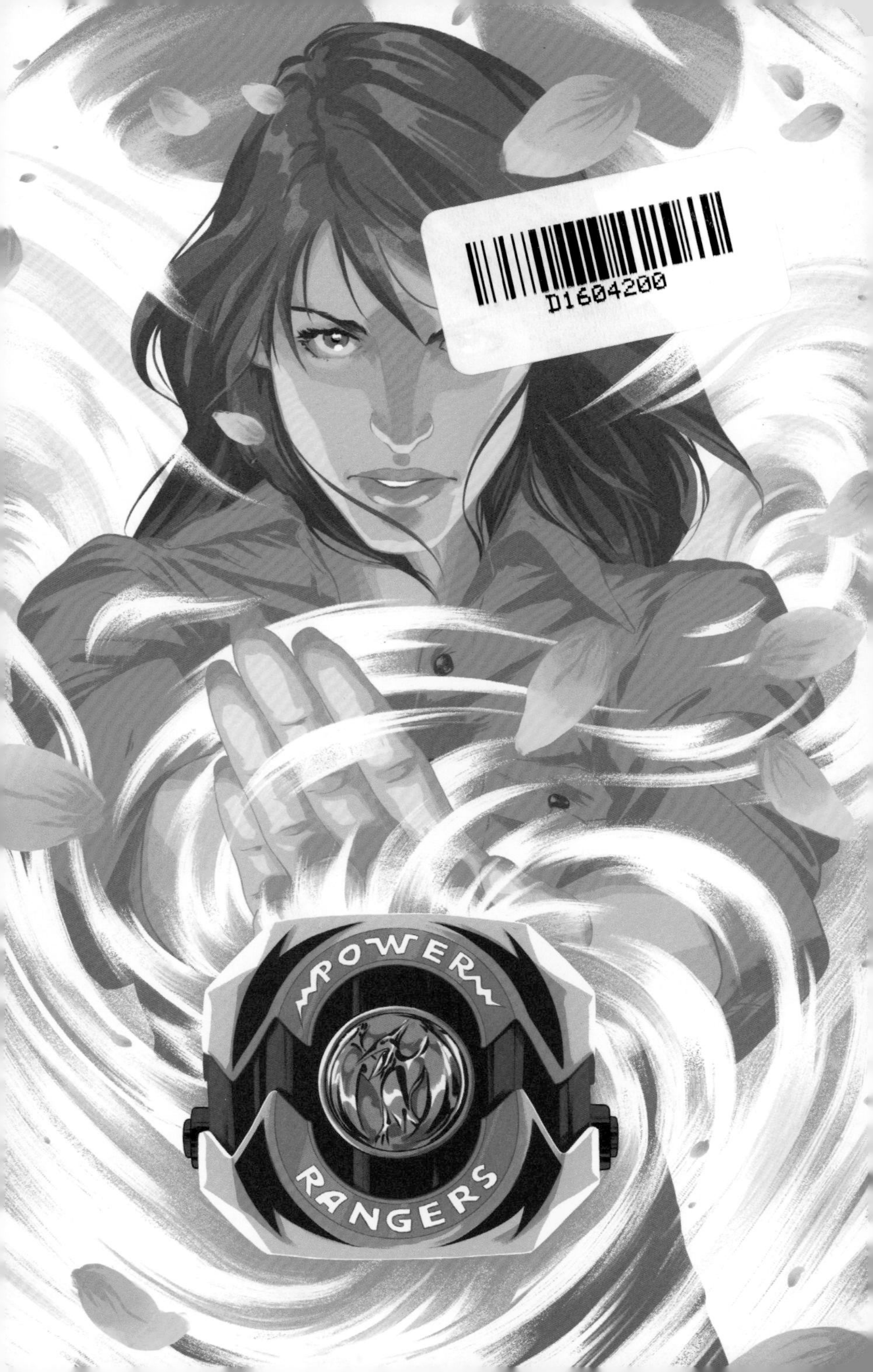
POWER
RANGERS

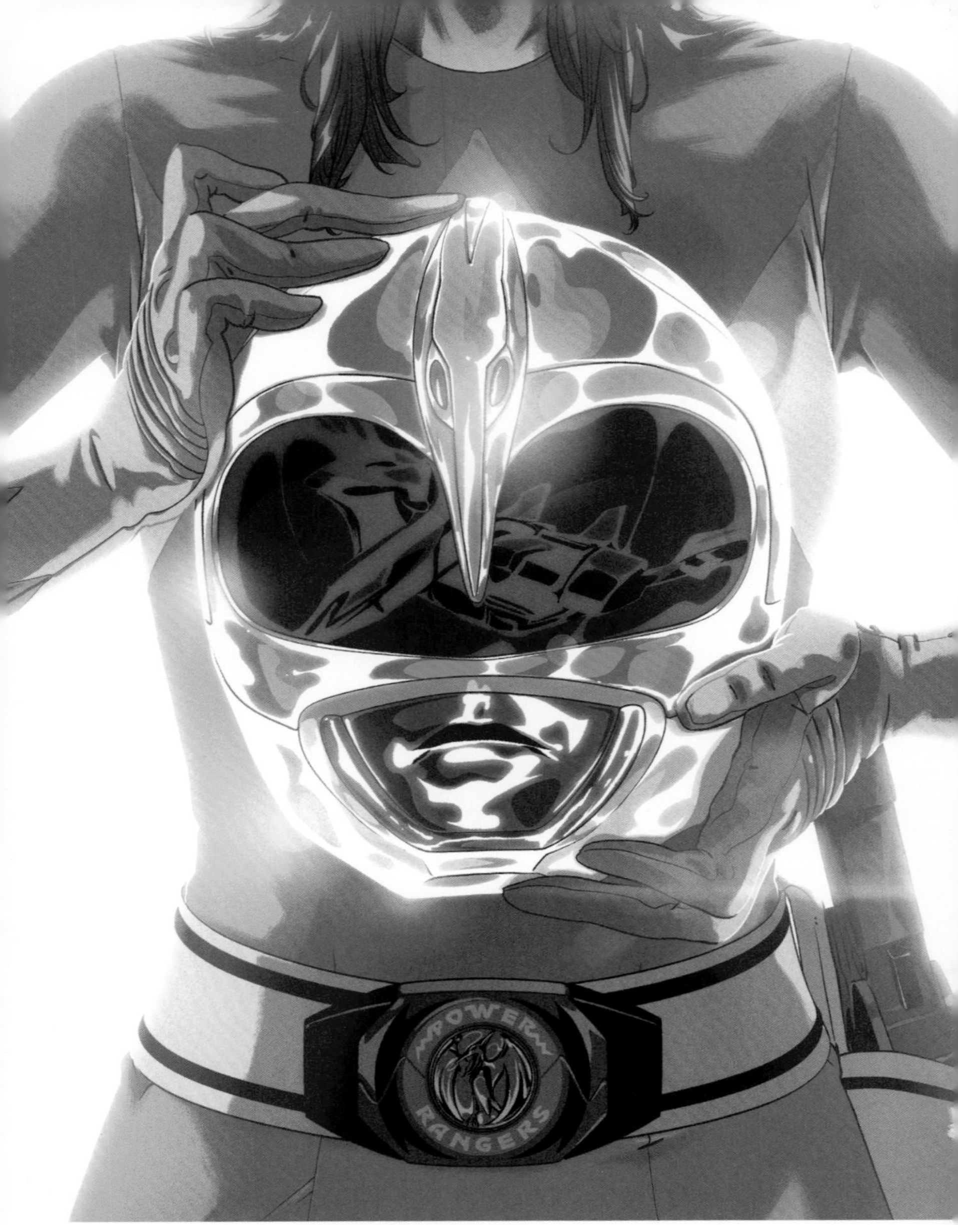

PROPERTY OF:

____

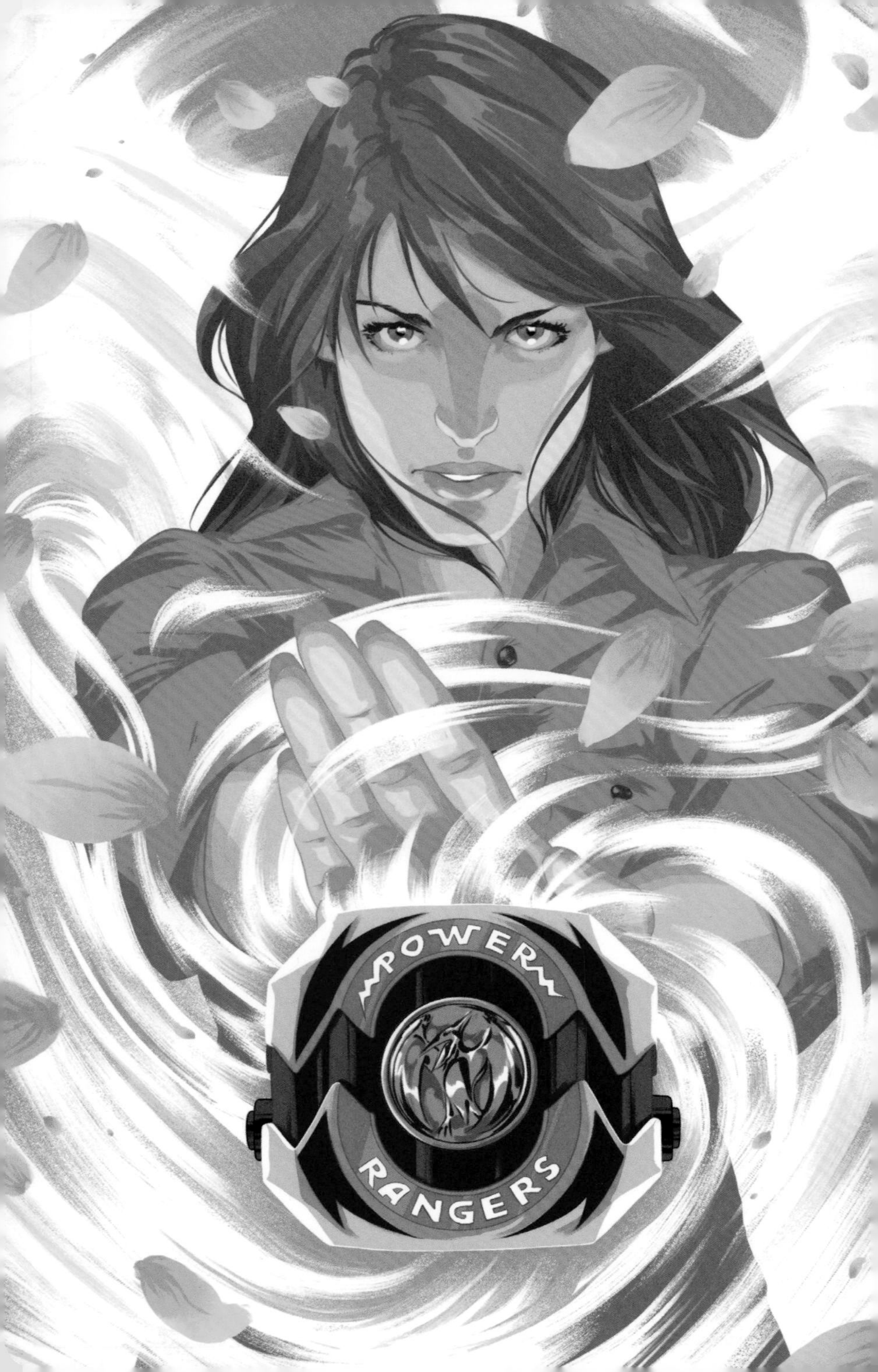
POWER
RANGERS